Let Her Go

A. Carys

A. Carys

The characters and events portrayed in this book are fictitious. Any similarity to real persons, living or dead, is coincidental and not intended by the author.

No part of this book may be reproduced, or stored in a retrieval system, or transmitted in any form or by any means, electronic, mechanical, photocopying, recording, or otherwise, without express written permission of the publisher.

Copyright © 2024 A. Carys

All rights reserved.

BOOKS IN THIS SERIES

Of Doors and Betrayal

The Pickpocket and the Princess

The Master, My Wings, Our Service

'Cos This Is How Villains Are Made

A Circus of Wonder

A Sentence to Death

A Deal With The Devil

Let Her Go

The Three

Queen Rory, The Banished

A. Carys

Let Her Go

DEDICATION

My lecturer has three Daleks on his desk. Legend.

A. Carys

CHAPTER ONE

Walking from the small cottage I share with my husband to the palace is a short journey on a good day, but being eight months and two weeks pregnant makes the journey feel a whole lot longer. It's a curvy, but flat path, so it isn't too bad to walk, but when I reach the grand staircase in front of the palace, I sigh. These stairs have become my nemesis, and it takes all of my strength to haul myself up the first couple.

It takes a while, but I finally make it to the second to last step. I must make a sound of discomfort as two guards rush over and help me up the last step.

"Thank you, both of you."

"No problem Mrs Tyrer. Would you like us to get Mr Roark?" asks Ollie, the guard who's holding onto my right arm.

"No. Absolutely not. He'd blow a gasket if he knew I'd wandered here by myself. If you could just help me to the War Room that would be great."

"Of course, Mrs Tyrer," Liam, the guard on my left, says as they escort me to the War Room.

"How many times have I told the both of you to call me Lily? Mrs Tyrer makes me feel old."

Surnames here are a funny thing. I know that in other worlds and realities, it's common for newlywed wives to take their husband's surname. To change their name on every single official document they have just so that people can identify them as a married couple. I also know that sometimes the husband takes their wife's surname, but that doesn't happen here. Our surnames are dictated by the kind of *Gift* we have, which then tells people what House we belong to. Our surnames represent who we are, they are our identity and changing them wouldn't make sense.

Children are given the appropriate surnames once their *Gift* presents itself, but that doesn't mean they belong more to one parent than they do to the other, it just helps them come into their identity more rather than them having a name that doesn't match who they are.

I am of the Tyrer line, so my surname is Tyrer. The Tyrer line has the *Gift* of Matter. We can sense the very molecules and atoms that make up the world and people. We can use our Gift to build and replicate. It's quite the unique *Gift*. My husband's *Gift* is telekinesis, which is quite common. The Roark line is a strong, known for its excellent military service and protection of those on any front lines. They are a powerful House with a lot of sway in both the palace and the Board of Representatives. Our baby will be given one of these surnames once their *Gift* presents itself, so they'll go by their first name for the first few years of their life.

The walk to the War Room passes quickly as the large wooden doors come into view. The boys help me to the door, opening it for me as well before Robert Mauder spots me. He gets up from his chair and comes over.

"Thank you, boys," I say to them as I take Robert's hand.

"Anytime, Mrs Tyrer," they say simultaneously

before walking away.

"I have told them so many times to call me Lily, Mrs Tyrer makes me feel old," I repeat to Robert with emphasis on my name and feeling old.

Robert chuckles. "Don't ever lose your spirit."

Robert helps me to a chair. He pulls it out from under the table and waits for me to sit in it, before tucking it and me into the table. He then hands me a plate.

"Since when do you serve breakfast at Board meetings?" I ask as I pinch a pastry from the top of the pile.

"Since today. Figured that, since I was making everyone meet at ungodly hours, breakfast was the least I could do," he explains as he comes and takes a seat at the head of the table. "Where's Magnus?"

"Showering when I left. I had to get out of the cottage, Robert. Mag has been extra doting lately and while it's nice, I felt like I was suffocating this morning."

He nods. "Well, if you need someone to come walk with you who isn't your husband, have a guard come and find myself or Lesley."

"Thank you, I'll keep that in mind," I say as I start tucking into the fruit I'd popped onto my plate.

Minutes after our conversation finishes, the War Room starts to fill up. Every time the door opens, I look over to it until I find the man I'm looking for. Magnus, my husband, slips into the room. I watch him walk around the crowd, his head on a swivel as he searches for me. When his eyes lock onto me, he sprints over to the chair I saved for him. He doesn't waste a single second as he starts asking me a thousand questions about where I went this morning. This then turns into a lecture about not leaving the cottage without him. Thankfully though, Robert starts the meeting moments into Magnus's lecture.

"Thank you all for coming so early, matters regarding the *identified citizens* have escalated," he says, which has everyone passing worried glances at each other.

"What do you mean by escalated?" Myrtle Wyran asks.

"The citizens we identified as the instigators of the absurd uprising attacked a Royal convoy last night. Luckily, it was just the Ceremony Carriages and horses being returned to the stables and storage, but we're classing it as an escalation of behaviour which means it's time for us to take protective action to ensure the safety of the general population."

"What are the—"

The doors to the War Room burst open and Lewis Enver runs in, closely followed by four guards. Robert stands up, pushing his chair back to the point where it nearly topples over, and rushes over to Lewis. He dismisses the guards after a few hushed whispers before bringing Lewis to the head of the table.

"A vision," Lewis says, and Robert gestures for him to speak. "A vision of a prophecy. War is coming and we must hide the Queens of House."

"What do you mean? What will happen to the Queens of House?" I ask, sitting up in my chair.

Altaine isn't run by one leader. While Lesley Amet is the overall Queen of Altaine, the head women of all of the Houses are also entitled Queen. They, alongside Lesley, run the country. I, myself, am a Queen, but my House is small so I'm not a major Queen. There's seven major Queens and seven minor Queens.

"You, Lily Tyrer. You are a part of the prophecy. Your child will bear a child who will save us all. She will be the chosen one, the lost child who will save us from those destined to try and tear us apart."

"Lewis, please explain. Please give us more information," Magnus begs and Lewis's eyes gloss over as he starts to see more of his vision.

"Your daughter will be born early. She will then be transported elsewhere to ensure her safety. Her first-born daughter will save us, but the rebels know, and they'll try everything to stop us."

The room erupts into conversation. Everyone starts murmuring about what is going to happen, I try to listen in on what they are saying but I can't seem to focus on anything other than the panic is rumbling through me. Nausea bubbles in my stomach as I reach out and grip onto Magnus's hand. I squeeze it as hard as I can as he tries to coax me back into the room, back into reality. But the panic is too much and before I know it I'm being lifted out of my seat and onto the floor. The cold of the tiles bites into the bare skin of my back as I continue to hyperventilate until the darkness ebbing at the edges of my vision takes over completely.

CHAPTER TWO

On orders from Doctor Omen, I spent the two days that followed the meeting in bed. But Robert and Lesley are holding a country wide public address today and I refuse to miss it.

I call out to Magnus, and he rushes over to help me out of bed. I waddle my way to our wardrobe and change out of my nightgown. I pull on a soft, light orange dress and pair it with a grey cardigan. I don't change my slippers, keeping them firmly on my feet even when Magnus asks if I need his help changing them for actual shoes. I make quick work of pinning my hair back before grabbing a couple of pieces of jewellery to complete the outfit.

"You ready to go?" Magnus asks as he pokes his head through the bedroom door.

"Yep," I say, collecting my purse before walking over to him. He offers me his hand, which I accept as we head to the front door.

We slowly walk along the stone path, following it to the palace. When we reach the grand stairs, Magnus helps me up them. It takes a whole lot longer than it did a few days ago, the difference now being a feeling of dizziness that's been coming and going throughout most of the day. Oh, and the fact that the baby is making their presence known by kicking the hell out of my stomach.

When we reach the top, the guards open the palace doors and observe silently as we enter. We walk through the halls until we reach the ballroom. Everyone has gathered inside of it, the Queens, King Robert, Lewis Enver, Nixon Mauder, Myrtle Wyran and Jason Kastell. We make our way over to the crowd and Robert begins the briefing.

"Lesley and I will make the initial address. We'll be taking four questions from the crowd before ending the address. We want to keep it short since we don't want to give the rebels a chance to cause any incidents. We know they're planning something, so we don't want to give them time to act impulsively," Robert says, and everyone nods. Despite the fourteen Queens being the overall rulers of the country, Robert is the one we all look to for guidance, for support. We look to him to know how the people of Altaine will respond.

"What about Lily? If the rebels know that the baby will be the beginning of our saving, they might try something to get Lily and the baby out of the way," says Myrtle, pointing out the obvious. Magnus's grip on my hand tightens in a mixture of worry and comfort. I squeeze his hand just as hard in return.

"In the line-up of the balcony, Lily will be kept toward the back, but will still be in the line of sight of the audience," Robert turns to look at me. "We cannot and will not risk your life, or your child's life, Lily. But myself and Lesley feel that it's important the rebels see that we are still united. We refuse to let them scare us into submission."

I nod as I move closer to Magnus, craving comfort. None of this was how we wanted to spend the last weeks of my pregnancy. We were ready to spend it in a little bubble, just the two of us until our baby graced us with their presence, but none of that is possible anymore. And as I stare down at the citizens who have gathered to hear what the King and Queens have to say, I feel sick. I feel robbed and right now I want to hide. I want to curl up under the duvet in our cottage and stay there until the baby comes.

"Welcome, everyone. Thanks to all of you who could make it in person today, but also welcome to those listening through the new radio system. I'm beyond ecstatic that it's up and running," Robert says, addressing the audience. "Today's gathering was called so that myself and your Queens can announce a couple of regulations that will be coming into force in the next week. These regulations are not meant to be callous, and we're not putting them in just for the fun of it. They're being brought in because of the rise in credible rebel threats to our country,"

The crowd murmurs, members of the public look at each other and share concerned glances. But in the midst of a basically stationary crowd, I catch sight of people shuffling and pushing through small gaps. I nudge Magnus and he bends down, giving me his ear.

"The crowd. I think there are rebels here now," I whisper as Robert starts explaining the new regulations.

"You sure?"

I nod. "People are shuffling, trying to get out of the crowd. I can feel the vibrations of their steps. It's like they're desperate to get out."

Magnus nods before grabbing a guard's attention. They whisper before the guard carefully disappears back into the palace. Magnus retakes his place at my side as I give Robert's speech my full attention.

"The fourth and final regulation we will be putting into place is the increase in guard presence around the cities and streets of Altaine. Guards will be doing spot checks on Identification Papers and will receive new training on identifying replicas and forgeries. This is all in the name of keeping you all safe. The last thing anyone wants is death and injury caused by thes–"

A loud boom from the far wall of the palace makes everyone stumble and the surprise cuts Robert's speech short.

A. Carys

CHAPTER THREE

"REBELS," someone yells.

Rough hands grab me and pull me back into the palace. I look up and see Magnus. He looks scared as he guides me to the safety of the ballroom.

Robert, all the Queens, Myrtle, Nixon, Lewis and Jason follow closely behind us. We all cower as Nixon and Queen Rosalie take up a protective position at the front of the group. They each clash their fists together before taking up a stance with their fists raised in front of their chests. Instantly, I feel their Gift working. Drowsiness bubbles inside of me and Magnus notices because he gestures to Samuel Omen. Samuel has been my doctor throughout my entire pregnancy, and since Omen's are the only bloodline not affected by Blockers, he comes over and takes hold of my hand, using his *Gift* to support both myself and the baby.

Blockers. Nixon Mauder and Rosalie Mauder, of House Mauder, are able to block and stop someone else's *Gift*. They hold their stance until the commotion outside stops and the guards who leapt into the action come back inside.

"Your Majesties, there are people outside in the courtyard who have requested to see you," the guard standing by the balcony doors says timidly.

Curious glances pass between us, and no one moves until Lesley gives a nod. Rosalie and Nixon take down their defences and everyone sighs at the sudden rush of their abilities coming back to them. Samuel stops his *Gift* but doesn't let go of my hand as Magnus takes hold of the other.

Everyone moves back towards the balcony. We line up behind the railing and look down to find two people looking up at us.

"Good morning, Your Majesties. What a lovely speech you gave, King Robert, but we have come to inform you that your regulations will not stop the Righteous. We have a path that has been laid out to us, shown to us from the stars themselves. We bypass your power filled bloodline by being one of the Righteous," says the woman, as she raises her arms up to the sky, almost like she were worshipping it.

"What is a *Righteous*?" Lesley asks.

"To be a Righteous you must be chosen. You must forgo your *Gift* to become powerless, to become a part of the Righteous you must be willing to choose between the regime and freedom. To become equal with all is what it means to be a Righteous," the man explains.

They're quite unsettling. The looks on their faces make my skin crawl and I wish they'd look at someone else, but their gazes are pinned on me. I remove my hand from Samuel's grip, placing it on my stomach. I gently rub, feeling comforted by the action, and in response the baby kicks. The people in the courtyard seem to follow my hand and their gazes become transfixed on my stomach.

"The baby will try to destroy the Righteous movement, but we will indoctrinate them first. We will turn them against you, and we will become unstoppable."

Darkness rolls over the courtyard which has us all gasping and looking around. When the pitch black clears, the two are gone but their warnings are seared into my mind.

"Robert," Nixon calls out, his voice laced with panic. We all turn to Nixon and see Lewis having another vision. His eyes have rolled back into his head, and he looks like he's having a seizure.

Lewis has always been unfortunate when it comes to his *Gift*. His *Gift* is extremely strong and that comes with complications of its own. Samuel rushes over to Lewis. They mutter to each other before Nixon lifts Lewis into his arms. They leave, disappearing to somewhere within the palace.

"He'll be okay, won't he?" Hattie Ayre asks.

"He should be fine. For now, let's start working on how we can defend the palace and Lily," says Lesley as she gestures for us to move back inside the palace.

CHAPTER FOUR

I groan as I waddle toward the bedroom divider curtains.

After the attack, and our strange conversation with the two that call themselves the Righteous, Magnus and I were moved into the converted loft space at the top of the palace. We've got a private bedroom that is closed off by a gorgeous set of lace curtains. The rest of the area is all open plan and I've been working hard to make it look, and feel, extremely homely. I've hung a lovely set of fire lights across the gap between the floating bookshelves. I've also hung up our wedding sketches and added three vases of flowers across the various surfaces.

I push aside the curtains and head over to Magnus who's washing the dishes from breakfast.

"Mag, I think we need to call for Samuel," I say as I lean against the back of the sofa, cramps in my lower belly rendering me immobile for a moment.

"What's going on? Is the baby coming?" he asks, dropping the dishes and grabbing a tea towel to dry his hands. He comes over and rests a hand on my back, rubbing gentle circles as another cramp hits.

"Oh goddess," I groan as the cramp gets more intense, one of my hands shoots to the bottom of my belly as I fold in the middle slightly.

"Okay, I think we need Sam." Magnus helps me back to the bedroom. He helps me onto the bed and props up the pillows behind me for support. "I won't be a minute, okay?" He kisses the side of my head before rushing out of the room.

I wait for what feels like forever before Magnus returns. But he doesn't just bring Samuel with him, Rosalie and Lesley come as well. They both rush to my side and grab my hands just as another cramp hits. I squeeze their hands as I try to breathe through it and they both say words of encouragement.

Once the pain subsides, Samuel sits on the bed next to me and starts examining me. He uses his *Gift* to test my blood, take my temperature, monitor my heart rate and blood pressure along with the baby's heartbeat. Once he's finished those exams, he moves on to timing the length of the contractions. They start off quite far apart, Sam timing them at about fifteen minutes apart before they slowly decrease to eight minutes apart. At this point, Magnus has climbed behind me so that I'm resting against his front. He's periodically massaging my shoulders and muttering sweet nothings in my ear every time he feels I need reassurance.

"I hate this," I murmur as another contraction hits.

"Down to six minutes apart," Samuel says, looking down at his watch.

I cry out. "I can't do this, I– this hurts too much."

"I know baby, but just think that once this is over we'll have our baby in our arms."

"But for how long? If the palace is attacked again then we have to do as Lewis said. We have to give them away to another reality," I cry, tears collecting in the bottom of my eyes as all the emotions hit me at once.

"We'll have time with them, I'll make sure of it. I won't let them take our baby right away," he says as he places a kiss on the back of my head.

Silence fills the room again and we all sit and wait as the contractions get closer and closer together. When my contractions reach three minute intervals, I start feeling this overpowering urge to push despite Samuel telling me not too. But the urge is too strong, and in the end, Samuel uses his *Gift* to help temporarily relax me so that I don't push before I'm meant to.

"Okay, contractions are at sixty seconds in length, so you're going to need to push now, Lily. Are you ready?" Samuel asks as he moves and bends my knees before moving them apart.

I nod and adjust my grip on both Lesley's and Rosalie's hands. Samuel counts me in for each contraction and every push. He has me push for ten before stopping and taking some deep and relaxing breaths. Samuel coaches me through this repetitive cycle and as he says the baby is close to being born, I feel like I've been pushing forever.

"Come on, baby. One more push and they'll be

here. Our baby is nearly here. Come on sweetheart," Magnus encourages as I rest against him, set on not pushing again. "Come on, we'll do it together. Three, two, one,"

Magnus pretends to push with me. When Samuel tells me to stop, an ear piercing cry fills the room. I sigh with relief and rest my head fully against Magnus. I let my eyes close while Samuel deals with the baby.

"You did it baby, I'm so proud of you. I'm so incredibly proud of you," he whispers into my ear. I smile as tears still stream down my face.

"A healthy baby girl, congratulations to both of you," Samuel says as I open my eyes. He's holding our baby in a towel, all freshly cleaned and no longer crying. He gently places her in my waiting arms.

I look down at her and the rest of the world just seems to disappear for a moment. My baby is in my arms. She looks so delicate, so sweet and precious. I gently run a finger over her cheek, and she makes a soft gulping sound.

"She's so squishy and soft," I mutter, and Magnus's hand gently strokes the back of her head.

"Our baby girl," he whispers. I turn my head, leaning to the right and carefully press a kiss to Magnus's lips.

"What do you want to name her?" I ask him.

"How about Everleigh?"

I smile and reposition myself again so that I'm resting comfortably against him again. "Everleigh is lovely," I mutter.

"We'll leave you guys to get settled for a moment, but I'll be back to check up on you in a little bit. That okay?" Samuel asks as he clears the used towels and replaces them with clean ones.

"Yeah, that's fine. Thank you, Samuel," I say as my focus remains on the little girl in my arms.

My heart feels so full as I look at my daughter. She's got a head full of the most beautiful light brown hair and when she opens her eyes, all I can see are the features of her that look like Magnus. But then the thoughts of everything that is going to happen in the immediate future crash into me like a tidal wave.

"I don't want to give her up, Mag."

"I know, I know sweetheart, I don't want to either. But don't think about that right now, just focus on yourself and Everleigh."

I nod and look back down at my daughter, fully ready to make the most of all of the time we have together.

CHAPTER FIVE

The week after Everleigh's birth flew by.

"Are you ready baby girl?" Magnus asks as he takes her out of my arms and cradles her to his chest. She babbles and tries to grip his shirt with her little fists.

Today is her christening. Christening in our reality is a way of connecting the child to the country and to the Goddess that our country was founded by. Tiana wasn't actually a Goddess or a myth, she was as real as myself and Magnus. She is the founder of Altaine, but we refer to her as the Goddess because she made Altaine a safe haven for the newly *Gifted*. And in our everyday lives, we hope that she will guide us into doing what is right and also help keep us from as much harm as possible.

"Are you ready my love?" Magnus asks me.

I nod.

"Yep, let's go," I say and take hold of his free hand.

We slowly walk down the stairs, being careful of Everleigh shifting too much and also myself after being extremely sore from the birth. When we reach the bottom, we head for the ballroom.

Upon entering, we find everyone waiting for us. The Queens are decked out in their prettiest gowns, Myrtle is wearing her favourite jumpsuit, and the men are all in varying shades of the same suit. We smile at everyone and say brief *hellos* before heading over to Carla, a lovely lady who has been baptising the children of Altaine for many years.

We greet Carla with the same *hellos* and introduce ourselves to her. By the time we turn around, everyone has taken their seats and is waiting patiently for the ceremony to begin.

"Welcome, friends and family and thank you for gathering here with us today to celebrate the baptism of Magnus Roark and Lily Tyrer's baby girl," Carla says, gesturing to Everleigh. "What is the given name of your child?"

"Everleigh," I say.

"And what is it that you ask of me today?"

"We would like for Everleigh to be baptised in the name of the Goddess," Magnus says, and I nod in agreement.

Carla opens her leather bound book, the cover inscribed with the title. Unfortunately, the title was lost in the old language of Altaine, but the text on the inside was redone sometime within the last two hundred years to allow for more modern audiences the ability to read it.

"You have asked for your child to be baptised. In doing so you are accepting the duties of teaching her your faith. It will be your responsibility to help her keep her way, to stay on the path that is right and clear. You will teach her how to love, respect and protect the people in her life, as dictated and taught by the Goddess herself. Do you understand the role of what you are undertaking?"

"We do."

"We do."

Carla nods, placing down the book and dipping

her thumb into the small metal cup next to her. She then brings her thumb up to Everleigh's forehead and presses gently against her skin. Her thumb hovers there for a moment before she pulls back and picks up the book again.

"Everleigh, the Altaineian community and country welcomes you with great excitement. In the name of our Goddess."

Everyone murmurs *in the name of the Goddess* in response, and Carla nods, signalling the end of the ceremony.

Celebrations begin almost immediately. The chairs that the guests were sitting on have been moved to the side of the room. Everyone is dancing and coming over to say hello to Everleigh. Magnus and I don't join in with the dancing, we just sit on the loveseat that's been set up at the edge of the dancefloor. I rest my head against his shoulder as we look down at Everleigh, trying to soak up as much time with her as possible.

I move my head so that I'm looking up at him. "I love you, both of you, so much."

He smiles. "I love you, Lily, and I love you, Eve.

And I'll do all I can to keep you both safe."

CHAPTER SIX

In the two weeks that follow the christening, we begin to draft up plans for emergency drills in case the Righteous decide to attack.

Things within the palace have been tense over the last few days. It's taken Lewis quite a while to recover from the vision that he had after the public address. But yesterday, he finally felt up to getting out of bed and managed to tell us about the vision he had. It was a powerful one, one that he had felt coming on hours before it happened. Like I've said before, his *Gift* is extremely powerful and this vision showed him, not only when and what will happen when the Righteous attack, but it also showed him how we can keep Everleigh safe.

"Will we ever see her again? See her first steps or

hear her first word?" I ask Lewis.

Myself, Magnus, the other Queens, Robert, Myrtle and Jason have gathered back in the War Room to hear what the vision Lewis had entailed.

"You'll see her again, yes, but you won't be there for any of her milestones, not even ones in her adult life."

My nose burns as his words register and tears gather at the bottom of my eyes. "I– wha–"

"We won't be there for her eighteenth birthday? Or her wedding? Or the birth of her children?" Magnus asks and I feel the arm that he has wrapped around my shoulders tense.

Lewis shakes his head. "I'm sorry, truly I am, but in order for her to remain safe, and for the prophecy to play out uninterrupted, you will miss out on Everleigh's life. But that doesn't mean you won't ever get to meet her."

"When will we?"

"I don–"

"Please Lewis, tell me. When will we meet her again?"

He sighs but looks me dead in the eyes as he says,

"She'll be thirty four when you meet again."

Tears start falling and I lean my head against Magnus, crying silently. *We'll miss thirty four years of her life. Thirty four.*

"I know it's not what you wanted to hear, but it's an important part of her, and our, journey as a country. The prophecy cannot be fulfilled unless she is in another reality. She must be kept separate from this world, well out of harm's way."

"What happens if she develops a *Gift*? There'll be no one to guide her," Robert points out which has everyone nodding and murmuring.

"You needn't worry about Everleigh developing a *Gift*, she will be a Tyrer, features and all but she won't have the *Gift*. Her children, however, will be *Gifted*."

Grandchildren. We're already talking about being grandparents and Everleigh isn't even a month old. My mind hurts and my emotions are all over the place. Normally, Envers do not tell others the details, especially vivid details, of the visions they have. It's heavily frowned upon in their House. But they sometimes give cryptic readings. It's dangerous to give out a lot of details because a lot of the time people will go out of their way to change the course of their fate, but that's not how it works and that makes people angry. But the information that Lewis is giving us is vital for us to prepare a safe outcome for Everleigh. He's not telling overly sensitive details which are meant to be kept private.

"I– I think– I think this is all too much for me right now. The information about her life. I don't want to know anymore, please," I say as Everleigh shifts in my arms, stirring, but not waking.

Lewis nods with a sympathetic look. "Then we can move on to securing her safety. The way out of the palace and into the reality she'll call home for a while. Any ideas?" he says and moves to the side of the chalkboard.

Robert rises from his chair. "I have an idea," he steps up to the board. "If we can pinpoint the exact reality we want to send her to, then we can work out a way for her to be monitored. Rachel, do you still have agents across the realities?"

She nods. "Yes. Most recently I have secured agents in a reality I think would be fitting for

Everleigh. A beautiful planet, normal people. No magic, no gas lamps and ink-dipped pens. A modern world with, I think the words were electronic technologies. She'd be more than safe and well taken care of."

"And do you have agents who could have a hand in where Everleigh is placed?" Magnus asks.

"Yes. I could get her placed within the area in which we leave her. There are procedures put in place to help keep babies safe and I think we can use that to help ensure Everleigh has a bright and happy life."

I nod in agreement, despite the ache in my heart.

"Anna, would you be willing to be the one to open a doorway for us to transport Everleigh when the time comes?" Lesley asks.

Anna Amet, a doorway opener. A doorway can take someone from their current position to a room further across the palace, or it can take them to another reality. Their *Gift* is powerful but temperamental; unless you're Anna Amet though. She has mastered the art of control when it comes to the doorways she opens, and I wouldn't trust anyone else to get my daughter to safety.

"It'd be an honour to help."

"Good. So we have a place and how to get there. Now we need to practise, run a couple of mock drills so that we know what to do in case of an emergency," Robert says while writing on the chalkboard. "Then we'll work on what to do with ourselves when the attack happens."

CHAPTER SEVEN

The days tick by slowly, and the quieter the Righteous become, the more on edge we all begin to feel.

We've practised what we will do with Everleigh come the attack, and we've also figured out where we will all go for our own safety.

"How are you feeling?" Magnus whispers.

We're lying in bed. Everleigh is between us, napping after her last feed.

I shrug. "Could be better. But I'm making sure to soak up as much time with her. I don't want any regrets when the time comes."

He smiles and nods before looking down at Eve.

"How are you feeling?" I ask him.

"I'm doing okay. Just taking it day by day."

We lay there for hours. Both of us drift in and out of sleep, only waking up when Everleigh stirs and reaches for us. We properly wake up at about half four in the afternoon. Magnus disappears down to the palace kitchens while I pick Everleigh up and take her to the balcony. I take a seat on one of the chairs we put out there and I let her rest against my chest as I look out at the sunset.

Sitting here, all of my problems and heavy emotions disappear.

"I love you baby girl. Don't ever forget that. But at some point you'll stay with new parents who'll look after you until the time for us to meet again comes. But I want to give you something before you go," I carefully lift her from my chest and rest her on my legs. I reach up and take off my necklace, the same one that was given to me by my mother who was given it by her mother.

"This necklace is a gift from me to you. It's something for you to keep with you while you grow up, a promise, if you will, of us reuniting. It's actually a key, I know it's funny shaped, but it's still a key. My mother never told me what it would unlock, maybe it doesn't unlock anything. But I want you to keep it, to have it as a piece of your real home, a place you will one day return to."

I clasp the necklace around Everleigh's neck, adjusting the chain to make it fit her better. She babbles, smiling, and her little fist closes around the key.

Thudding footsteps behind me has me twisting in the chair. Magnus quickly comes into view, his face filled with panic.

"What's going on?" I ask just as the palace seems to shake and a loud boom sounds over to my right.

"They're here."

CHAPTER EIGHT

Another roar of commotion catches my attention.

I stand up with Everleigh in my arms and I see them. What looks like a small army is marching their way up the main road to the palace, and they're periodically blowing things up as they move ever closer.

"L, we need to go now," Magnus says as he runs over to the sofa where our go-bags have been sitting for the last few weeks.

I move inside the room and grab the blanket I made for Everleigh while I was pregnant. I wrap her in it before grabbing her little bag and following Magnus. He takes us through the palace as it shakes from the force of the attacks.

"Ayre's. Come on, quickly," he encourages as we

enter the ballroom and head straight for the west wall.

The palace shakes again, and we nearly topple over, but thankfully the shaking stops before we fall. We make it to the west wall and Magnus makes quick work of pressing the painting into the wall. The wall rumbles and shakes as the bricks start to move and fold in on themselves to reveal a passage. We rush inside of the passage and Magnus make sure that the wall closes behind us.

Once he's sure the wall is secure, he beckons me to follow him down the passage. We head straight forward, then turn right, another right and then a final left before we head down a long staircase. Everleigh shuffles and fusses in my arms, but we make it to the bottom of the stairs without incident.

"Thought they'd already gotten to you," Lesley says as she emerges from another passageway.

"Not yet. Where's Robert?" I ask as the four of us keep moving.

"Already down there. The Queens are waiting with a protective circle in case of a breach."

"Is Anna ready?"

"Yes. She's been prepping nonstop for the last

twenty four hours. I think she knew it would be sooner rather than later."

We reach the lower levels of the palace. The lower levels were closed off many years ago because there wasn't any need for them. Thankfully, they are the perfect place to facilitate our one way ticket out of the palace and into the underground city.

"Magnus, say your goodbyes now and then head into the tunnels," Lesley orders as he guides me into the middle of the protective circle.

Magnus comes with us, his eyes focused on Everleigh. I watch him closely, noting the tears that are building in his eyes as he whispers to our daughter. She looks up at him and reaches her fist out to him. He lets her grip onto his finger and his tears fall when he leans down to kiss her forehead.

"I love you, little girl. You be good now, and I'll see you soon," he tells her, and I have to look away to stop myself from crying, but it's no use as the tears fall freely.

"We need to go, now," Anna says as she begins to open the doorway.

"I'll see you in a few hours," I say to Magnus

who has now turned his attention to me.

"Make sure she's safe," he murmurs as he leans in for a kiss. It's a sad kiss, full of loss, desperation and longing.

"I will," I say as we pull apart. "I'll make sure she has the best family."

"Lily, we've got to go right now," Anna says as the walls around us rumble, and shouting can be heard.

I step away from Magnus and through the doorway. I turn around instantly and take one last look at my husband before Anna closes the doorway.

CHAPTER NINE

Anna takes hold of my hand as soon as she drops them from the doorway-summoning position.

"Come on, Rachel gave me instructions on how to reach the safe place."

I nod and pull my gaze from where the doorway was. I follow after Anna. We walk through a densely wooded area. We clamber across dangerous tree roots and up a hill before carefully walking down the other side. We finally reach a sign that reads, *Welcome To Amwin, Please Drive With Care*.

"Is this it?" I ask.

"Yes. But the place we are to leave her is further inside the town," she says and carries on walking.

"What do you mean?"

"There's a safe place for babies to be dropped off,

it's all anonymous and the babies are taken into care after they are collected."

I hesitate, looking down at Everleigh as I begin to doubt the decision to leave her in this world.

"I know this is scary and I can't imagine how you are feeling right now, but I want you to remember that you'll see her again. This isn't a permanent goodbye."

I take a deep breath and nod before letting her guide me through the woods. It isn't long until we come across a large brick building. There's two frosted windowpanes encased in red metal which have been attached to the front of the building. The sign at the top of the building reads *Amwin Fire and Rescue*. My steps slow down as we approach what I assume to be the front door and I hold Everleigh closer to me.

"We need to place her here, knock on the door and then walk away. They'll look after her. Rachel assured me this is the place for her to receive the best kind of chance until she's called upon."

I swallow thickly. "I can't do this."

"Yes, you can. You're strong, Lily, you can do this."

I shake my head. "I can't, I– I really can't."

"You can, just follow my lead," she says as she guides me over to the blanketed bassinet. She moves me so that I'm standing close enough before pressing down on my back, urging me to place her down. I carefully bend and unfold my arms when they hit the mattress. I pull my hands from beneath Everleigh before covering her more with the blanket.

Anna takes Everleigh's bag from my shoulder and places it on the hood of the bassinet. I step back after placing one final kiss on her forehead. I turn my back, not being able to look at my baby as I leave her with strangers. As I leave her in a strange world, so far away from her actual home.

As I walk away, I hear Anna knock loudly on the door of the building. It takes everything in me not to turn around, but a doorway quickly appears in front of me and Anna ushers me through it.

CHAPTER TEN

A man opens the door to the fire station.

He does what he is instructed to. Upon hearing a knock on the door, he has to wait thirty seconds before opening the door. He checks the bassinet and sees a baby, bundled up in a thick blanket.

"Baby?" asks one of his colleagues.

"Yeah."

"Do you want me to call it in?"

The first man shakes his head. "No. Let me do it," he says as he picks up the baby along with the bag that was left on top of the bassinet.

He heads back inside, the baby securely in his arms and reaches for his phone. He opens it and clicks the phone app. He clicks the *recent callers* button and picks the fourth number. As it rings, he puts it to his ear and waits.

"You're going to be okay little baby; I'm going to help find you a good home."

"Thomas?"

"Hey, Elena, I've got a baby here. Was left outside in the bassinet."

"Okay, give me ten minutes and I'll be with you."

"See you soon."

The call cuts and Thomas looks down at the baby again.

"You hear that? Miss Elena is coming to help you. She's the very best at what she does, don't you worry 'bout a thing."

ABOUT THE AUTHOR

A. Carys is a self-published author from Portsmouth, United Kingdom. Other than spending 90% of her day writing, she also loves to crochet, read, and take photos of her family's cats.

Printed in Great Britain
by Amazon